LESBIAN SEX

EXPLICIT DIRTY EROTICA SHORT STORIES

CARLEE SHOMAN

plicit Press
Erotica Fiction

CHAPTER 1

ESMERALDA

THE SOUND of people moving around in the house is distracting, but twenty-one-year-old Lisa, home to celebrate this birthday milestone with her family, cannot lift herself from the bed to close the door. Her hands are already on her vagina, under her tight panties, the tip already digging into her. Lisa's eyes are closed now as her fantasy envelopes the room and she is no longer in her own bedroom, the sounds around her gone, and her vagina being touched by a familiar lover's own delicate fingers. Lisa raises her knees as she sends her finger deeper into herself.

Esmeralda appears in the doorway. The twenty-some-thing-year-old Latina housekeeper almost drops the laundry basket in her hands at the sight. The sight of Lisa masturbating stops her in her tracks and she watches the scene play out for a while. Lisa is so gone that she doesn't register the presence in her doorway. Esmeralda enters the room and very slowly, she closes the door. Still, Lisa doesn't stir; no idea that she is no longer alone in her bedroom. Slowly Esmeralda approaches the bed, the laundry basket still in her hands. She is almost on the bed when she realizes that she might want to put the clean clothes she's carrying down.

With her hands free, Esmeralda is on the bed. Lisa almost jumps off of it as she realizes its presence. They exchange a look, Esmeralda's is lust and curiosity, Lisa's is an embarrassment that soon becomes a dirty *why-don't-you-finish-what-I-started*. Esmeralda goes immediately for her lips and is kissing Lisa as though they've kissed a million times before. The kiss is deep, warm, passionate, and familiar. Lisa can't help kissing her housekeeper back. Her fingers go deeper into her vagina, which now erupts spontaneously at the presence of a hot Latina in the *not-a-fantasy-anymore* scenario. Both women exhale long through their noses as the sensations of the kiss play havoc on every nerve ending in their bodies.

Esmeralda lands lengthy fingers on Lisa's legs. She traces circles, half-circles, and every other round shape she can imagine as she works herself up from Lisa's ankles to her thighs, the parts between her legs where her underwear cuts a clean boundary, and then her fingers are on the panties, over the hand that Lisa has lodged under the fabric. Esmeralda's hands move over every part of her body, not shying away from her cunt even though Lisa's fingers have monopolized the sweet-scented vagina. Just the idea that foreign fingers might soon be inside her has Lisa digging deeper into her cunt in preparation for this.

Lisa kisses Esmeralda hard now as the idea settles upon her that she will have an aided climax. Her hands too are all over Esmeralda, touching every part of her body that is available through her uniform. The skirt is generously short and so Lisa makes the focus of her fingers on Esmeralda's thighs, ass, and cunt. Unlike her, Esmeralda doesn't stop Lisa from settling on her own vagina.

There is no resistance when Lisa's fingers grope clumsily for a minute and then pull Esmeralda's panties down almost to her knees. There is no resistance from Esmeralda when suddenly and without warning Lisa sends a finger into her moist vagina.

After letting her play for a bit, Esmeralda is again in control, removing Lisa's vest and sucking her breasts. The warm wetness of her mouth makes Lisa shiver as Esmeralda sucks on each of her breasts in turn. The nipples in her mouth grow, Esmeralda loving this response. She sucks hard, pulling as much of each of Lisa's perfect tits deep into her mouth. Then her sucking becomes gentle kissing on the entire surface of the mounds, Lisa confused and enthused, excited by the multiple sensations.

There is no resistance now when Lisa's panties are removed. She helps by wriggling out of them, her legs almost over the top of her head now as Esmeralda makes quick work of discarding the cottons. Firm hands grip the inside of Lisa's thighs, parting them. The fingers dig into her thighs and then find her pussy, swelling now in anticipation of contact. Still, Esmeralda keeps teasing her with the possibility. The possibility alone expands Lisa's clit, the pink perfection drawing Esmeralda in, her face moving almost involuntarily towards the middle of Lisa's legs. The legs widen also involuntarily and Lisa spreads them wide for the convenience of Esmeralda and her agenda.

At last, Esmeralda's fingers are on Lisa's clit, pinching the bud with tender conviction. Fingertip after fingertip teases the entrance to her hole, now a wet cove. Her fingers move in deeper and deeper, the space is too inviting. One finger at a time Lisa's pussy is penetrated, the process making her want Esmeralda even more. The way that her vagina is being touched reminds Lisa repeatedly that women know exactly how to touch each other. She can't help but to surrender herself completely to the more experienced Esmeralda. Esmeralda enjoys the novice underneath her touch, weaving a sensual tapestry now in her cunt.

Removing her fingers now she feeds Lisa the taste of her own pussy while taking her mouth down so that she too can get a taste. Esmeralda takes Lisa into her mouth, immediately sucking deep and hard. While sucking she sends her tongue deep into the ready vagina. Lisa lets out sultry squeaks as her pussy is being devoured. Esmeralda nibbles on the cunt, tugging on the clit with her teeth, then her lips. Lisa thrusts into Esmeralda's mouth and Esmeralda aids her lust by clamping down hard. While munching down, Esmeralda repositions herself so that her own pussy is now over Lisa's face. Lisa now is able to suck on her wet pussy as well.

They eat out each other's pussies, both women doing on the other what they would like done to themselves. There are so many ways to have your pussy eaten out, and all of these ways play out on the two cunts in the room. Both women are now totally ignorant of the house and its activity, everyone planning a party for the girl getting a very intimate early birthday present. They start to explore each other's cunts even deeper now with their fingers, their tongues facilitating the additional invasions. They no longer limit themselves to one finger at a time as they pull each other's cunts apart.

Lisa reaches for her overnight bag when she eventually manages her breath and a gap. The bag is on the floor next to the bed. She reaches into the bag and pulls out a large rubber dildo. It's an interesting tool, the kind that extends from a central handle into two rather large, very real-looking dicks. They both laugh at the tool for a minute and then

Esmeralda takes it from her. She teases Lisa with it, running it along with her mouth, down between her breasts, and then between her legs. The scented oil on the bedside is the only lubrication on hand. The smell of vanilla fills the room as Esmeralda runs the oil over the dildo and then rubs it over the entire shaft.

The dildo is then inside Lisa, slowly making full entry. Esmeralda is gentle and patient. Her patience is unnecessary, Lisa wanting the entire tool inside her quickly so that she can focus on the woman giving her the pleasure. The tool moves in and out of Lisa's cunt, moving deeper in after every partial extraction. Lisa's hands are on Esmeralda, touching her breasts, pulling her face into her own for a deep kiss, and then wrapping her arms around her neck so that Esmeralda has her head on Lisa's chest, her eyes on the tool she is still working in and out of her juicy pussy.

Lisa finds Esmeralda's pussy with her own fingers. The space is wet, warm, and sticky. Lisa's fingers are inside the deep tanned pussy quickly. She fucks Esmeralda as intensely as her delicate fingers can manage; nothing like the massive dildo Esmeralda is plowing into her pussy. But she makes up for size with pressure and Esmeralda is soon gasping almost as loudly as she is. Each time either of them gets carried away, they remind each other of the party planners moving around the house and the fact that Lisa's super-conservative parents should be back any minute.

The second head of the double ended dildo isn't lubricated, but Esmeralda eases it into herself, also needing a more physically intimate positioning with Lisa. Lisa's half is lodged deep inside her pussy, so Esmeralda moves closer and closer to Lisa, the end of the rod inside her pussy going deeper and deeper the closer she gets to Lisa. By the time they are close enough to each other for their breasts to touch and their lips to settle comfortably on each other, both women have eight inches of rubber inside their wet pussies. Arms around each other, they begin to make love.

The fillers in their vaginas are a perfect complement to the intimacy playing out on their lips. They obsess over each other's breasts, kissing, biting, and sucking on each other with a tenderness that belies the thrusting in the area of their cunts. Their vaginas dealt with, they concentrate on the soft intimacy that makes a woman the best lover for another woman. They know how to touch each other. They know where to touch each other. Most importantly, kissing being the most important part of their lovemaking, they both know that there is no speaking required here. The moment is best enjoyed in silence.

Again, it is the intimacy of their fingers inside each other that they crave. So they make this connection and the dildo is discarded. Both women touch the other, as they would like themselves to be touched. Each woman recipro-cates the desired touch so that both of them are in perfect hands. Their fingers find each other's depths and they let their lips come together as their fingers send pulses through each other's cunts, climaxes close. They lie next to one another, close enough for maximum reach into the vagina, but also so that they can lay flat on their backs while kissing.

They start to climax almost simultaneously. Lisa's fingers stir the inside of Esmeralda, Esmeralda's fingers doing the same. Her climax is closer, and Lisa digs deeper and harder into Esmeralda. The Latina reads the signs and sinks her own fingers deeper into Lisa. She turns to face her and then gets on top of her, releasing Lisa's hand from her own cunt. Esmeralda looks down on Lisa, her full weight on her now as she makes the intention of her hand very clear. She uses the other hand to wipe the sweat off Lisa's brow before coming down and kissing her, her fingers beating the inside of Lisa's cunt rigorously.

Under Esmeralda's full weight, Lisa edges on to climax. She wraps her legs around the woman who has turned her vagina into a tidal pool. The waves sweep over her until she is lost to the pleasure. Lisa's hands are above her head, her fingers in her hair. She starts to fuck Esmeralda's hand as it pulls her orgasm from the far reaches of her vagina. Loud exhalations are the only sign that the orgasm has begun, Lisa ejaculating streams onto Esmeralda's hand, the fingers of which refuse to dislodge from her cunt until the absolute last minute.

Lisa digs deep into Esmeralda's pussy, already wet as it starts its involuntary pulses toward the climax. The fingers inside her spicy cunt run circles up and down its walls and Esmeralda lets out a series of subdued pants as she starts her epic climax. Lisa tries to silence her with her lips when her panting gets too loud, but the attempt is only effective while their lips are together.

Lisa makes her efforts more determined so that Esmeralda is soon in the throes of her orgasm, her body almost contorting around the fingers inside it. She holds Lisa's hand in place as her pussy extracts the last moments of pleasure from Lisa's fingers. They stare at each other for a minute before reality brings the room back into focus...

CHAPTER 2

EATING OUT...(DINNER FOR TWO...)

TINA IS in a state when the new waitress, Saffron, opens her office door without knocking. She gives the twenty-year-old, who really doesn't know any better, a stern look, and then motions with her head for her to leave. Instead, Saffron closes the door and then locks it.

Tina looks puzzled, not used to not having her orders, spoken or not, disobeyed. She is, after all, the owner of this damn restaurant, and Saffron is nothing but a doe-eyed waitress. Tina doesn't even know what the girl does when she isn't here.

Saffron removes her apron as she makes her way to where Tina is sitting behind her desk. She puts it on the desk and then places her hands on Tina's neck after rubbing them together. She tells her boss to just relax and enjoy it, that she has the experience to make it all better. Tina is just too tired and frustrated to contest; and as soon as Saffron's fingers are working on her neck and then her scalp, Tina isn't about to stop the young girl, immediately loving it.

The delicate fingers move in deep circles over the entire surface of Tina's head and Tina moves her head to the back. This extends her neck and Saffron can't resist moving her fingers onto Tina's neck. The touch isn't firm now, but a gentle fluttering as Saffron strokes Tina's neck lightly with the tips of all her fingers. By the time Tina realizes the sexual element it's too late. She opens her eyes to find that Saffron is staring at her with lusty eyes. Tina's pussy beats rapidly, heating up at the possibility of this new experience. Saffron looks to where Tina's neck becomes her chest and then her breasts. The shirt she wears allows for a great view of her tits from where Saffron is standing behind her. Before she can stop herself, her fingers are tracing along the mounds on her boss's chest. Tina's had it for the day, so she just closes her eyes and surrenders to Saffron and her youthful recklessness.

Tiny fingers work on the buttons of Tina's shirt until her bra is exposed, along with her flat, firm belly. Saffron comes around and turns the chairs so that she is standing in front of her boss. She goes under the shirt and unhinges the clasp on Tina's strapless bra. Then she places the bra on the table just before she places her lips on Tina's breasts. She can smell that Tina is one of those women who spray some perfume on her breasts.

She sucks on her large nipples, taking care to send her desires through Tina using her tongue. This is all very new to Tina but she loves it. It feels right. It feels fucking awesome and Tina wonders why she hasn't been with a chick before. But she could just be so frustrated that any physical release is welcome.

Saffron continues to work on Tina's tits as she places a hand on her thigh. She doesn't want to move too fast in case she scares Tina, or worse, offends her. But Tina's thighs are warm and inviting, and soon enough Saffron's hand is disappearing under the tiny pencil skirt covering the parts of Tina she wants.

She gets to Tina's cunt quickly. With just two flat fingers, she rubs the surface of the cunt, covered by the lightest lace. Saffron presses a little harder on the clit and then tries, still over the lace, to locate the snatch. Finding it, she nudges into it with the tip of her finger, pushing lace into Tina's pussy. Tina murmurs, watching the door, but with her eyes closed; not wanting to believe this.

Then the panties are pulled away and the same two fingers slip under the elastic. Tina's pussy is perfectly shaven. Saffron can't even feel any telltale stubble. It must be a professional wax job. She moves her fingers up and down the smooth surface, enjoying the feeling of the clit between her fingertips.

She finds the hole again, and again she goes in, a little deeper now that the lace isn't barricading the way into Tina's cunt. Saffron fingers Tina slowly with just half of her finger as she kisses away at the scent of expensive perfume on her breasts, a perfume that smells and tastes like watermelon and vanilla.

Tina's legs part as widely as her tight skirt will allow. Saffron encourages the skirt a little further up her legs so that they have more space to move. Then she removes her finger and helps Tina rid herself completely of her panties. They slide all the way down to Tina's ankles and then past her heels and off. Saffron takes a minute to appreciate Tina's pussy with her eyes. She pulls Tina closer without forcing her to stand. She goes between her legs with her head and sends her tongue into Tina's cunt. The pussy is tight, probably nerves. But still Saffron gets her tongue inside it. She licks hard and deep so that Tina is soon moist and throbbing. Then she licks the clit rapidly while sending two gentle fingers deep inside Tina who has now quite forgotten the stresses of the evening.

With a hand on each of Tina's thighs, Saffron creates more space between her legs for her head. She is inside the pussy with her tongue again, drinking everything that Tina's vagina has to offer. Saffron eats out the pussy with the hunger of youth and the skill of a well-established lesbian.

She is determined to make all the bad things go away.

She licks the inside of Tina's pussy with great precision. It's almost impossible for her to be getting so deep with her tongue but she does. Tina isn't sure what to do with herself, holding Saffron's head, and then grabbing onto the chair. Saffron understands her confusion and explains herself by just digging harder into Tina's cunt, now dripping impressively.

Saffron comes up to breathe. But this doesn't mean that she needs to give the pussy a break. Three of her fingers now dig deep into Tina, and Tina has lost her mind, pulling her hair out of its neat bun and shaking her head from side to side. She pushes her head hard into the back of the chair and bites her lips as Saffron fingers her harder and harder.

Then Tina's legs close and she squeezes the shit out of the hand between them. But Saffron is not deterred. She circles the inside of the wet pussy as hard as she can, unable now to move her fingers in and out of it. Tina cannot believe the skill that is being meted out on her cunt. Saffron is fast proving to be a very good hire.

She has a very animated orgasm. Her thighs crunch down powerfully on Saffron's hand and then her legs try in vain to straighten, succeeding only in kicking Saffron hard. But the girl takes it, staying exactly where she is, her fingers still active inside Tina so that her orgasm is completed. Tina comes forward and then arches back a few times while she is escorted back down from the cloud she is sitting on.

When her legs relax enough Saffron carefully removes her fingers from inside Tina. Then she goes for her pussy with her mouth while using the fingers that are wet with the juices of Tina's pussy to find her own cunt. Saffron fingers herself slowly as she licks, sucks, and nibbles Tina's cunt, inside and out. Tina is satisfied but senses that she could do this forever.

Once Saffron has her own orgasm, eating out Tina's cunt until she does, she blows warm air onto Tina's cunt. Then her fingers are back in there. She starts off with just one, fusing their juices as she feels the tightness of Tina give way. She adds a finger and plies the pussy until it gives way a little more. Soon she is up to four fingers and Tina is really feeling the stretch. Her eyes are open now, watching her cunt and also checking for shadows under the office door.

Then Saffron obstructs Tina's view of her cunt with her head. She finds her clit with her lips while working on her snatch with the four fingers. The fingers part and then come back together inside Tina. It takes a while for her to get used to this massive stretch. Saffron keeps going, occasionally nibbling on Tina's clit with her teeth. The bites are both hard and soft, and sometimes it feels like she has plucked her clit right off. But then she licks it to bring it back to bloom and Tina knows that her love flower is still intact.

When Saffron moves her head and Tina can once again see her pussy she cannot believe her eyes. Saffron has managed to get her entire hand inside Tina. She reaches down so that her hands are both on Saffron's arm, threatening to pull the hand that is quite tightly engaged with the inside of her pussy. Saffron warns Tina that it won't be very pleasant if she just yanks it out. She insists that Tina just relax, and enjoy it. She encourages her to give it a minute. It doesn't take much to convince Tina.

With her legs raised over Saffron's shoulders now, Tina tries to relax her muscles by breathing deeply, but every millimeter that the fist inside her moves sees her tense up again. She had no idea that a whole fist could fit inside her tight pussy, despite all the stories she's heard. This wasn't something that had ever appealed to her. Tina had always thought of fisting as a largely unnecessary discomfort.

But then her pussy adjusts and relaxes snugly over the fist. Saffron starts to move easier around inside her. She eases her hand as deep into Tina as possible. Then she pivots around inside her a few times before easing it back towards the outside world. When it seems she might pull out Tina begs her not to. So Saffron eases her fist all the way back up into Tina's willing cunt.

It isn't long before the fisting has gained momentum. Tina holds onto the chair with all she has as she is now being fucked almost offensively with Saffron's whole hand. Her forearm is soaked with pussy cum. It is gliding in and out with the gusto of any dick. But there is a feminine tenderness that makes Tina want more. She is no longer shy to ask for more.

Saffron gives it to her. She rams all the way up into Tina so that it seems her whole arm might be lost inside Tina's cunt. There is no rush. They couldn't give a fuck right now about the fact that the staff is waiting outside for Tina to do the cash-up. They are lost in this world that comprises for the most part now of just pussy and clenched fist.

When Tina is ready to blow Saffron finds her own cunt with her free hand. She works swiftly on her own clit so that she can meet Tina where she's at. Fucking her harder and harder with her fist, she finds the inside of her own pussy with four fingers. She digs the shit out of herself now, as it seems that Tina might beat her to the blow. But she doesn't, and the pair of them have a simultaneous orgasm of epic proportion. This is the kind of shit fairytales are made of.

Tina cannot move. She watches as Saffron moves her hand out of her cunt, slowly. She can see every centimeter as it makes its exit from inside her, coated in all the excesses of Tina's lust.

Saffron is also wet, her panties and her thigh, part of her skirt too, soaked in her own juices. After what feels like an eternity, her hand pops out of Tina's tiny cunt and the hole closes back to hide its treasure again. Saffron helps get her panties back up and her skirt adjusted. They check each other for signs of their deed and then escape into the washroom just off Tina's office. It's clear on everyone's faces when the two finally emerge that they know that the girls weren't just talking...

CHAPTER 3

ME AND MY COLLEGE ROOMMATE (FIRST TIME LESBIAN)

THEY SAY that you never forget your first time. I still remember Amanda, my college roommate. She and I would become more than roommates or even more than friends; we would have a bond that is more sacred than either of those. For a while we were lovers. It was my first sexual experience. Amanda took me to places that I had never been and to be honest, to places that I have not been since then. I am married and have two wonderful kids, but I often wonder what Amanda is doing these days and if she thinks of me as much as I do her.

I arrived at Memphis Polytechnic as a young student. I had never really been on my own. I had left the town I lived in a couple of times, but I had never been on my own. This was going to be a new experience. I met Amanda later in the day that I was moving in. From the beginning, she seemed to be almost too good to be true. I had a hard time thinking that I was going to have a woman like her care about me. I was surprised to discover that she was more than willing to help me. We struck up a friendship where I learned that she was the second of three kids; her older sister had gone to college so she had an idea as to what she could expect when she arrived. We became inseparable. Wherever I went, she would come along. Since Amanda was going to just stay at school, I asked her to come along with me so she could meet my family and so she would not be alone during the Christmas season.

The spare bedroom that we used for guests was currently under renovation. I suggested that Amanda could just sleep in my room. We had been roommates this long it was not like we had not seen each other naked. Amanda put her stuff in my room and settled in for the next two weeks. It was nice to have Amanda around, I felt at times like she was a sister to me as that was how close me and her were. If we were any closer, we would have been lovers. I was in the shower one day when Amanda came in, having to go to the bathroom very badly. I did not think anything of this, as I was going about my business when the shower door came open. It was Amanda. She had stripped naked and was coming into the shower with me.

Part of me was a little scared, as I had not been this close to a naked woman and there was a part of me that was wondering what the sensations that I was feeling were. I felt my cunt begin to quiver and I was on the edge of getting aroused. I had this sensation before but it was usually when I was around a person. Amanda looked at me and told me to just relax and let things go the way that they were supposed to. Amanda came over and kissed me on the lips. I felt like fireworks were going off inside of me and I was on fire. I felt a gush of liquid that escaped from my cunt and splashed onto the door of the shower.

I went and returned the favor and kissed Amanda back. Before I knew what was happening, we were sharing one of the most passionate French kisses that I had ever experienced. I had kissed a number of people but I had never kissed a girl. I was almost certain at this point that I wanted my first time to be with a woman. I had dreamed of being romantic with a man, but I also was in the moment and I wanted her. My parents were off shopping and there was no chance of them coming home. I was so hot for Amanda that I really did not care and actually hoped that they would come home, as the thought of them catching me having sex with another woman made me even hotter.

Amanda took her hand and began to work my slit over. I felt her fingers going inside of me, driving me to a point that I thought I would not be able to withstand much longer. I began to play with Amanda's nipples. She had her nipples pierced and the sensation of me playing with them caused her to get even wetter in her crotch than she already was. I wanted to take in all of Amanda and get her pure essence. Amanda and I left the shower and headed towards my room where we finished up with what we had been doing. Me and Amanda took a double-ended dildo that she brought with her and wound up fucking ourselves with it at the same time. I learned so much from Amanda in the two weeks that we were on vacation from school. We had a number of other encounters during the break that allowed us to become even closer

. . .

I do wonder if Amanda is happy in her life and also if things with me would have been different had we allowed our love for one another to grow even more than it already had. One day I hope that we cross paths again. I would sure like to be with her one more time for old time's sake and to taste her sweet snatch like I did when we were in college. I guess it is true you never do forget your first time.

CHAPTER 4

TASTY TONGUE

CANDY STARED AT HER SVELTE, naked body in the mirror. She wanted to watch herself masturbate as she touched herself in erotic places that only she knew. She had to go out and meet someone to spend the night with. Her hands slowly crept to her soft, big breasts to start fondling them. She watched herself in the mirror as her fingers alternately played with her nipples.

Her vagina started to get moist. However, she was not satisfied with her own fingers; she had to feel a naked woman's body against her own. She cursed under her breath and dressed up. She had been going frequently to this bar downtown because she was fascinated by Miley, the bar's lovely singer. She wanted to bring her home tonight and make love to her all night long. But Miley had a boyfriend and that was the problem.

When Candy arrived at the bar, Miley was giggling and necking with her boyfriend, Liam, There were only a few customers around because it was still early.

Candy sat beside the couple and intentionally brushed her big, luscious breasts against Miley's arm. Miley looked at her for a fraction of a second and continued playing around with her boyfriend, as Candy's pussy became even moister.

Miley's fresh perfume wafted to her nostrils and she ached to place her fingers between Miley's thighs. Candy could hear the couples' breathing rising an octave higher. She was hyperventilating as well.

Behind the cover of the shadows, Candy sensed Liam's hand inside Miley's undies, and her breathing stopped. How she would like to be in his place!

Laughing lustily, Miley pulled Liam and directed him toward the dressing room. Miley was horny and she wanted to have a quick fuck before customers arrived. Surreptitiously, they rushed into the dressing room and continued necking and petting, unable to control themselves.

Candy was horny as hell and wanted to watch them as she masturbated. The couple didn't bother to lock the door as they grabbed excitedly at each other, kissed, and fondled.

Liam propped Miley onto the dresser table and was running his fingers up and down Miley's vagina as he stuck his tongue into her mouth and savored her sweet taste.

Candy could no longer contain herself. She slowly slipped under them and started licking Miley's anus with slow deliberate movements of her tongue.

Liam and Miley were busy sucking each other's tongues and fondling each other that Miley thought Liam's fingers were doing that to her ass too.

The pleasurable sensation in Miley's ass started to build up and she moaned as the sensation included the area around her pussy. Liam's hands stopped when his fingers encountered Candy's tongue.

Startled, Liam and Miley looked down at Candy lapping Miley's pussy like a cat savoring its milk. Candy was already half-naked, caressing her tits with her free hand.

"What the...?" Liam exclaimed.

But Miley captured his mouth and continued fondling his rock-hard dick. Miley had never experienced a woman sucking and licking her pussy and anus, and she loved it. It was a totally different sensation. It was heavenly!

Candy's tongue on her vagina was exploring all those hidden nooks and crannies she had secretly wished Liam would discover. Only a woman could truly know what would pleasure another woman.

Miley scrambled down and knelt to take Liam's hard, pulsating penis into her mouth. Liam closed his eyes and groaned like a wild animal. Miley went on all fours, to expose her dripping vagina to Candy, who continued sucking her clit in measured, steady strokes until Miley was near explosion.

Then Candy inserted two of her fingers in Miley's pussy. Her fingers went in and out of Miley's pussy as she continued running her tongue up and down her clitoris. She was lying supine, her face below Miley's pussy, while her right hand was caressing her own moist and longing vagina. She wanted Miley to perform cunnilingus on her too.

Miley ran her tongue around the crown of Liam's dick, and then up and down his throbbing shaft. Then she took him into her mouth and sucked as she moved her mouth in and out of his dick.

Their movements became frenzied as lust overcame them and they responded to the burning need of their bodies. They were all over each other's bodies, caressing, fondling, and sucking whatever area their fingers and mouths were exposed to.

Liam grabbed the hair of Miley and was shoving his big, long tumescent penis into her mouth. Faster, and faster, he thrust his hips in pleasure, while Miley was writhing with the exquisite vibrations Candy's mouth and tongue were creating in her body. Miley had never experienced a woman's tongue in her pussy, and she loved every moment of it.

She moaned when Candy, increased the pressure of her fingers inside her vagina, in her G-spot just below her pubis, while Candy's tongue ran up and down her clit.

She moaned loudly as the waves of pleasure threatened to explode right then and there. She monetarily stopped sucking Liam, and this drove him crazy. He grabbed Miley by the waist, turned her towards him as he shoved his huge, angry penis into her, making her scream as her climax roared to life.

Candy was left clamoring for the fulfillment, her fingers not able to satiate her desires. She pulled a stool, sat on it, and spread her thighs to allow Miley's tongue the freedom to explore her vagina.

As Liam fucked Miley from behind, Miley sucked and licked Candy's pussy from her doggy position. They were all on the verge of their orgasms.

Miley came first, moaning and crying as she shuddered in unadulterated pleasure. Liam came next grunting happily as he locked his groin into Miley's soft bottom, and Candy came last as Miley lapped her juices with her tongue.

The noise of incoming customers in the opposite hall reverberated in the night.

. . .

"We've got to do this again," Miley spoke first, hurriedly covering her half-naked body. She loved Candy's tongue.

Liam nodded, still beet red in the face, he was still holding his nine-inch cock.

And all Candy did was to nod her head as her orgasm was still subsiding in her groin.

CHAPTER 5

WINNING HER OVER

I LAUGHED at Lucy's comment. "I'm never ever gonna be with another woman...I can't see myself doing that...Period." She was so convinced by what she was saying. I knew that I could make her eat her words. The only question was, would she allow me? Would she allow me but ten minutes to let her experience the things she could never experience with her boyfriend James?

"I'm not trying to be mean Lisa...It's just how I feel sweetie" she gave me a warm look as if trying to justify her statement, now that she'd played it off.

"I can change your mind, in five minutes I guarantee you," I blurted out and almost regretted it soon after saying it.

"What?" she gave me a curious look. Had she not heard me correctly? "What did you say?" she asked almost in disbelief.

"I said I can change your mind in about five minutes," I repeated assertively.

The next sentence that came out of her mouth left her even more surprised than it left me. My best friend Lucy had always been one who couldn't back down from a challenge. And what I'd just told her had seemed like the ultimate challenge to her.

"Fine, I'll give you ten. Ten minutes to convince me that a woman can pleasure me better than my man."

Was she serious? If she was then I was wasting time thinking about whether she was serious or not.

"Good, follow me then," I led her upstairs to my bedroom.

"Is this where the magic happens?" she joked sarcastically, still very unconvinced that there was anything I could do to win her over. But little did she know I was very persistent, and even though I didn't win her over completely, I would give it my best shot.

I invited her to get undressed since we didn't have much time for foreplay. She slowly got out of her clothes and laid in the bed naked waiting for me.

I parted her legs slowly maintaining a steady gaze. I could see that she was nervous, and decided to tease her a little, just to get her wet enough so she'd actually beg me to satisfy her thirst.

Slowly I brought my tongue down to her inner thighs and stroked her long legs from her knee all the way to her pussy, and then back to her knee again. Her body shook viciously as she struggled to control herself. Finally, when I brought my fingers to her folds, I found the most delicious surprise. She was dripping wet. I would have never known based on her cries that she had been struggling to maintain a serious face the entire time. That coy little vixen had been enjoying the tease all along, I thought to myself.

She yelped as my tongue made contact with her sweet juicy pussy. I parted her folds with my fingers, and teased the tender flesh of her pussy lips, blowing soft kisses against it, while giving her several slow long licks. Soon I developed a pattern and began moving my tongue repeatedly on her wet pussy, licking her tender flesh.

I finally moved upwards to her clitoris, took it between my lips, and tugged unto it softly. As I realized it, I quickly took it in yet again into my mouth, this time I massaged my tongue against her swollen bud, slowly at first but faster and quicker, releasing it occasionally to lap her juices along her pussy lips.

I was shocked when I heard her cry out for more. Her cry surprised me since she'd been quiet almost the entire time. Her voice was strained, as if she wasn't satisfied, she'd just die.

"Harder, please...please," her leg shook viciously as her fingers dug into the sheets. "Do you really want it...Really...?" I teased her by licking her pussy between my statements.

"Yes! Yes! Yes!" she moaned out breathlessly, gripping the back of my head firmly, forcing my head to remain in position between her legs.

Satisfied by her level of arousal I decided to increase her pleasure by introducing my fingers.

Her body tensed, as I penetrated her slit with three of my fingers.

"Oh God yes!" she cried out, as I began thrusting my fingers slowly into her temple of delight.

My tongue continued to probe her clitoris, sucking it lightly then increasing the suction on it, sucking it until it had swollen to almost double its normal size. As I pleasured her, her juices oozed out of her pussy, coating my fingers and tongue with her sweetness. I could feel my own arousal from the way her body seemed to react to my stimulations.

In and out I shoved my finger into her slit while pleasuring her with my tongue on her clitoris. Until finally there was a loud cry and she released, reaching her orgasm.

"I want to try to do you," she stated and we quickly changed position.

She was shocked when she saw how aroused I was. I didn't have to instruct her as to what to do, she knew exactly how to pleasure me. Taking my nipples into her mouth, she sucked and tugged unto their hardened picks, while her fingers massaged my throbbing clitoris. I moaned in pleasure, I wanted nothing more than to release onto her waiting tongue.

But I wanted her to do it on her own, I didn't want to force her into doing anything she wasn't comfortable with. Lucy finally eased my torture when she brought her tongue into my wetness, licking and sucking the tender flesh of my pussy. I bucked my pussy against her lips, as her tongue moved feverishly over it, licking and sucking at its juices. When she took hold of my clitoris I thought that I was about to ascend into heaven. Closing my eyes, I let out several loud ecstatic cries as his tongue swept through my pussy almost viciously.

My body spiraled out of control when she began darting her tongue into my slit, over and over. I could feel my arousal approaching at an immense rate. Finally, with a loud cry, I exploded my juices unto her waiting tongue.

"So good," she moaned lapping up my juices.

When she was done, she brought her lips to mine and kissed me passionately. Did I just win her over? From the way she was kissing me, I could tell that I probably did.

ABOUT THE AUTHOR

Carlee Shoman is an emerging erotica author of many erotica kinks and sub-genres. Be sure to check out other books and leave a review if this story got you hot!

Visit my blog at Carlee Shoman's Blog

Join my newsletter for the exclusive Carlee Shoman's Newsletter

Sign up for Free Stories from Xplicit Press AuthorsCandra Aubrey's Blog

Xplicit Press Author Updates

Like Xplicit Press on Facebook

Follow Xplicit Press on Twitter

Readers: I want to expand a few of the stories to see where the characters can be explored further. If there are any of the stories that you would like to read more about again, I'd love to hear from you!

Keep In Touch
Carlee Shoman
info@carleeshoman.com

www.ingramcontent.com/pod-product-compliance
Lightning Source LLC
Chambersburg PA
CBHW020814130626
46554CB00006B/2437